The Tree of Life

The Wonders of Evolution

The Tree of Life
The Wonders of Evolution

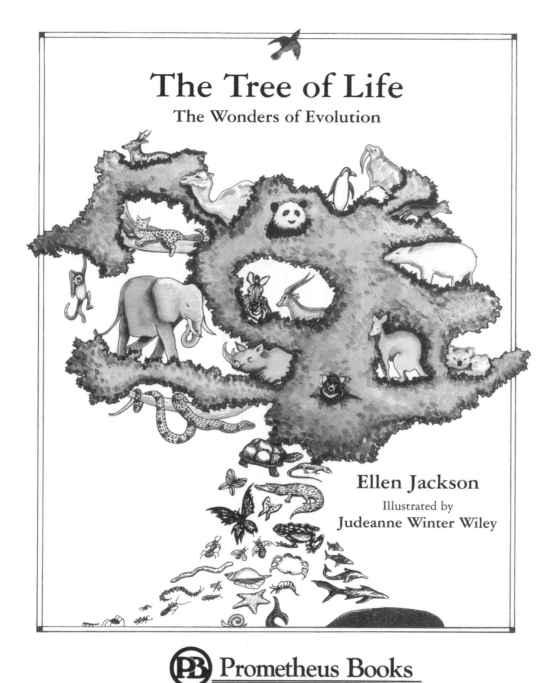

Ellen Jackson

Illustrated by
Judeanne Winter Wiley

Prometheus Books

59 John Glenn Drive
Amherst, New York 14228-2119

Published 2005 by Prometheus Books

The Tree of Life; The Wonders of Evolution. Copyright © 1993 by Ellen Jackson. Illustrations copyright © 1993 by Judeanne Winter Wiley. All rights reserved. No part of this publication may be reproduced, stored in a retrieval system, or transmitted in any form or by any means, digital, electronic, mechanical, photocopying, recording, or otherwise, or conveyed via the Internet or a Web site without prior written permission of the publisher, except in the case of brief quotations embodied in critical articles and reviews.

Inquiries should be addressed to
Prometheus Books
59 John Glenn Drive
Amherst, New York 14228–2119
VOICE: 716–691–0133, ext. 210
FAX: 716–691–0137
WWW.PROMETHEUSBOOKS.COM

11 10   6 5 4 3

Library of Congress Cataloging-in-Publication Data

Jackson, Ellen, 1943–.
    The tree of life : the wonders of evolution / by Ellen Jackson : illustrated by Judeanne Winter Wiley.
        p. cm.
    Summary: A simple explanation of the process of evolution, from the first appearance of "almost alive things" to the development of the millions of life forms that exist today.
    ISBN 978–1–59102–240–4 (alk. paper)
    1. Evolution (Biology)—Juvenile literature. [1. Evolution.] I. Wiley, Judeanne Winter, ill. II. Title.

QH367.1.J33 1993
575—dc20

                                    LC Number pending
                                    CIP
                                    AC

Printed in the United States of America on acid-free paper

To Shirley Morrison—Ellen Jackson

To my mother—Judeanne Winter Wiley

Note from the Author

During a recent trip to the library, I noticed that, while there were many books retelling biblical creation stories, there were relatively few books on evolution for younger children. Those books that attempted to explain evolution did so in a way that, though scientifically accurate, conveyed none of the wonder and excitement of this concept. *The Tree of Life* is my attempt to help young children understand the beauty and power of this great idea.

Obviously, a book for young children on this topic must leave out some complex details (for instance, the role of sexual selection as one of the driving mechanisms of evolution). The illustrations, also, must necessarily be somewhat abstract and suggestive rather than literal. Nevertheless, great care has been taken to maintain accuracy throughout, although some of the ideas have been simplified for this audience.

In the beginning days of the Earth,
all was silence.

Lightning and thunder crashed from the cloudy sky,
but there were no ears to hear it.

Torrents of rain splashed to the ground,
flowing into rivers, lakes, and oceans.
But there were no eyes to see it.

Nothing green grew on the craggy, grey Earth.
No flickering fish swam in the empty seas.
The Earth was a vast rocky land waiting to feel
the first breath of life.

But with every crash of lightning, the air, the water,
and the light were mixed together.
With every flicker and flash—
water and heat, light and gas danced together.
They mixed and mixed for millions of years,
holding together and breaking apart . . . until . . .

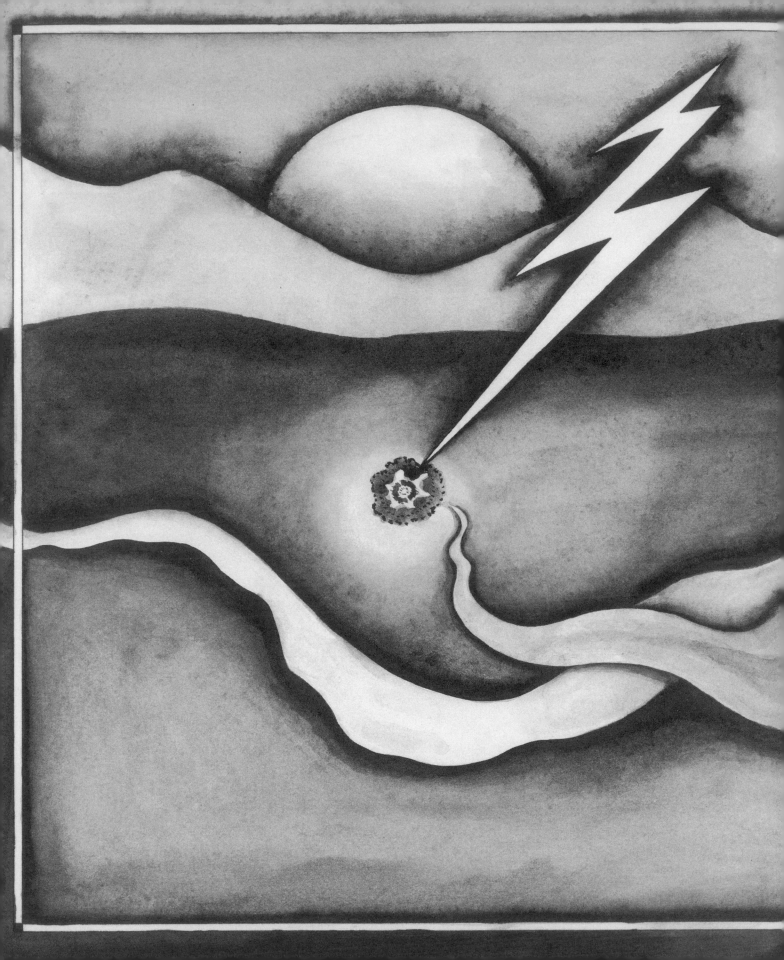

Something new happened.
There was a coming together of water and heat and gas
that was special. A bit of something very tiny appeared
for the first time. It wasn't a tree, a fish, or even a worm.
It was too new and too tiny to be much of anything.

But this something new was very special
because it was almost alive. This almost alive
tiny thing could divide in two again and again.
Each half of the tiny thing could then make
more of itself using the water and heat and gas
around it. It could grow.
And so it divided and divided.
Tiny bits of the new thing floated
here and there, dividing again and again,
filling the waters of the Earth
with copies of itself.
And each of the copies
divided and divided.

Did the new thing always copy itself exactly right?
The answer may surprise you. Almost always it *did*
copy itself exactly. But once in a great while,
not very often, a copy would be different
from the others.

 If the difference was harmful, the almost alive
thing that carried the difference could not
keep making copies
of itself. Maybe the
 difference
 made it
 too slow,
 too fast,
 too sticky,
 or too
 smooth. It would
 die or fail to
 reproduce.

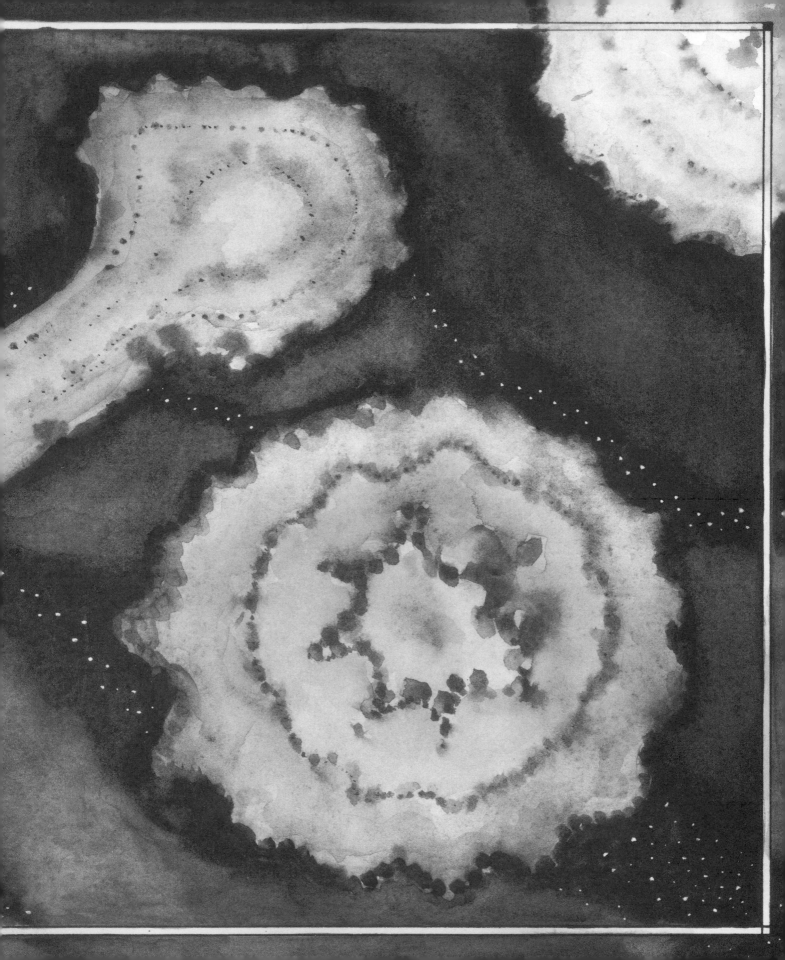

But some differences were helpful or good.
A good difference would make the new almost alive copy
better in some way. Maybe it could survive in colder water
or divide more quickly. Then the new copies that had the
good difference would be better at surviving.
More and more of them would come into the world.
More and more of them would survive.

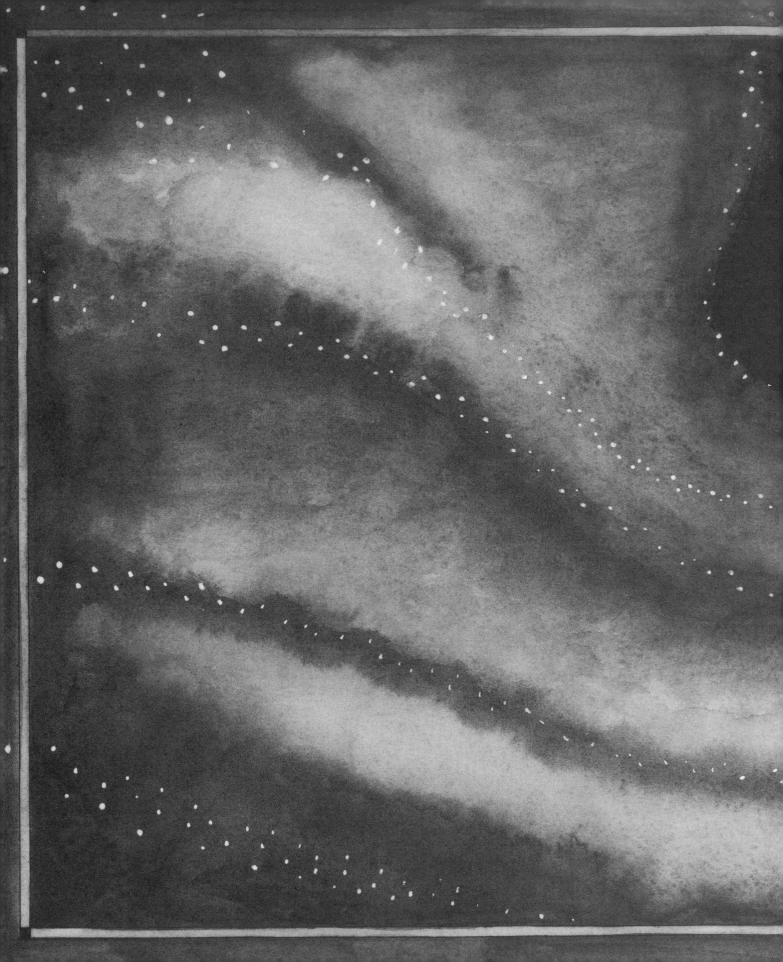

Millions of years went by. The tiny, almost alive things made copies that made copies that made copies.

A rainbow of beginning-to-be life-forms spread outward through the oceans. After millions of years, the new life-forms were bigger and better than ever before. Many good differences had occurred, and the tiny things that were changing and evolving passed these good differences on when they copied themselves. Many wonderful new kinds of aliveness appeared in the world.

Living things swam in the waters of the oceans. At first these living things were only tiny, microscopic bits. But as the copying and reproducing continued, bigger animals began to appear. Shellfish, jellyfish, and worms came first, followed by the fish. On the rocky land, plants took root and began to grow. All of these had come from those first almost alive things that had copied themselves over and over, changing in many different ways to create different kinds of life.

Then, after millions of years,
other marvelous changes occurred. Some fish grew
lungs to breathe and developed simple limbs so that
they were able to crawl out of the waters onto the land.
These were the amphibians.
Slowly, slowly other strange and wonderful creatures
came into the world—flying insects, reptiles,
and dinosaurs.

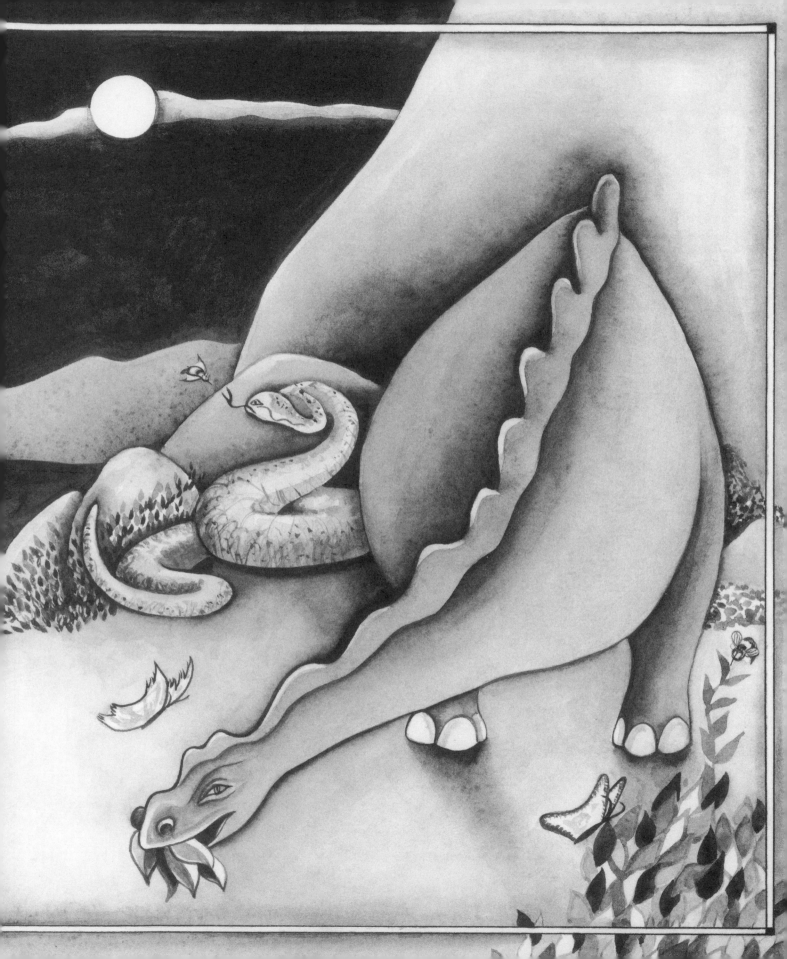

Everywhere the tree of life was growing.
The reptiles represented one branch of this tree.
From this branch came the mammals and the birds.
Some kinds of animals and plants prospered for a time,
then disappeared when their living conditions changed.
All of this took millions and millions of years.

At last mammals, reptiles, and birds of every form, feather, and beak filled the continents of the Earth. From a small mammal that looked like a mole or tree shrew came a group of animals called primates. At a time when great ice sheets covered much of the world, the first early humans appeared. They had evolved from an apelike primate.

These first humans walked on two legs instead of four, lived on the ground, and used stones as weapons. They fought for survival against cold and wild beasts. During the short, cool summer, they searched for nuts and berries to eat. During the winter, they hunted animals with wooden spears and knives of flint.

Everywhere antelopes and zebras,
deer with many kinds of antler, tigers,
wolves, foxes, and badgers jostled and
devoured each other, fighting for
room to live and raise their young.
The Earth bloomed with flowers.
All around, living things
fluttered, swam, and played.

Even today the tree of life keeps on growing. All living things are joined together by this wonderful tree that grew from the first almost alive tiny thing. The Earth is full of beetles and birds, redwood trees and whales, butterflies and baboons and humans. Life dances in the bodies and forms of all these creatures. It is a magic torch that has been passed down through the ages to all the living things on the planet. We will hold it awhile before passing it on to others.